OOPS!

OOPS!

POEMS BY **ALAN KATZ**
DRAWINGS BY **EDWARD KOREN**

MARGARET K. McELDERRY BOOKS
New York   London   Toronto   Sydney

MARGARET K. MCELDERRY BOOKS
An imprint of Simon & Schuster Children's Publishing Division
1230 Avenue of the Americas, New York, New York 10020
Text copyright © 2008 by Alan Katz
Illustrations copyright © 2008 by Edward Koren
Art direction and book design by Polly Kanevsky
The text for this book is set in Jigsaw.
The illustrations for this book are rendered in pen.
Manufactured in United States of America
10 9 8 7 6 5 4 3 2 1
Library of Congress Cataloging-in-Publication Data
Katz, Alan.
Oops! / by Alan Katz ; illustrated by Edward Koren.—1st ed.
p. cm.
ISBN-13: 978-1-4169-0204-1
ISBN-10: 1-4169-0204-X
1. Children's poetry, American. 2. Humorous poetry, American.
I. Koren, Edward, ill. II. Title.
PS3561.A745O55 2007
811'.54—dc22
2005032439

To my beautiful wife, Rose,
who's truly poetic from her head to her toes
—A. K.

And to my splendid wife, Curtis,
who, courageously, never made a bus fuss
—E. K.

WHOOSH!

The wind is blowing
quite a breeze.
The wind is blowing
on my knees.
The wind is blowing
its spring dance.
It tells me
I forgot my pants.

REAL-LIFE
SOAP OPERA

My sister was fascinated
by the underwater scene.
She asked, "When did we get a round TV?"
I said, "You're watching the washing machine!"

DON'T LOOK FOR
HIM ON THE WEB

Little Miss Muffet
got scared on her tuffet
while eating her curds and her whey.
But little Miss Snider
just sat on the spider
and snarfed on Miss Muffet's buffet.

FOUL BAWL

The score was tied.
Dave passed the ball.
I squeezed it with both hands.
I dribbled and then
shot it high.
A great hush filled the stands.
The ball went in!
Man, what a toss!
The whole team blew a gasket!
A perfect shot,
except that it
was our opponent's basket!

Two weeks went by.
Another game.
This time I stole the ball.
My hands were tense.
My chance had come
for glory after all.

I threw it hard.
I threw it fast.
As fast as it could get.
It wasn't blocked!
And yes, it rocketed
right through the net!

The crowd was mad.
The coach got sore
and sent me to my locker.
That throw was great,
he did admit—
but we were playing soccer!

This morning there's another game.
We'll win it in a rout.
It's baseball, and the coach said I
will surely play "left out"!

DON'T BE **1O-SE**

1-derful
2 see you!
Glad you could come
4 dinner!
But sorry,
we
already 8!

CRASH DIET

My mom drove us for fast food,
and the guy there had a cow!
The place didn't have
a drive-thru.
Thanks to Mom,
they
sure
do
now.

BITTER FOR CRITTERS

Hey, can we get a dog?
Can we get a cat?
Can we get a frog?
Can we get a bat?

Why, even for a teeny mouse
I've cried and begged and blubbered.

The only pets in this whole house
are the ants inside the cupboard!

DID HE TAKE A
MACBATH?

When Shakespeare was a little boy,
his parents thought him smart.
For every day he gave them joy
through wisdom he'd impart.
Such as the time he faced the bowl
and spoke a great decree.
He uttered from his wondrous soul,
"To pee or not to pee."

HIS ROYAL SLOPPINESS

I am the prince
of fingerprints.

Each thing I touch,
I smudge.

I got ink on
the windowsill.

And on the lamp?
That's fudge.

There's mud on
every doorknob

and paint marks
down the hall.

But don't blame me—
I've no idea

what's on the bathroom wall!

THE PENMANSHIP HAS
SAILED

My handwriting's really lousy,
and my **b**'s all look like **d**'s.
I never close my **o**'s enough,
though often close my **c**'s.
My **s**'s are like 5's, and so
my teacher's lost her cool.
Today we're gonna work on this
when I stay after school.

Lick lick lick lick lick.
Lick lick lick lick lick lick.
Lick lick lick.
Lick lick lick.
Lick lick lick lick.
Lick lick lick lick.
Lick lick lick.
Lick lick.
Lick.

STICK!

THE LOLLIPOP

HE EVEN HAS SUPER-VISION!

I'm sitting in the
principal's office.
But it's not scary,
it's cool.
Because, you see,
I'm the principal
and I run this whole school.

15

NO EGGS-AGGERATION!

I'm writing a love song
to eggs.
They don't have eyes,
they don't have legs.
They cannot sing,
they cannot dance.
You cannot keep them
in your pants.
But they're my friends,
is what I've rambled.
I love them so . . .
especially scrambled!

SHOW AND SMELL

I stuffed my lunch
in my race car—
salami and some soda.
It used to be a Chevy,
but it now is a
Toy-odor.

HAIR? WHERE?

Dad says, "You're giving me gray hair!"

At my behavior
he's often appalled.

But I don't see much
gray hair way up there . . .

looks more like I'm making him
bald!

ME

I have superpowers.
I can see through walls.

I can jump fifty feet into the air
when emergency duty calls.

I can swim the English Channel
and scale Mount Everest in an hour or two.

I can save the world with a wave of my hand.
But first . . .

would you please tie my shoe?

BROTHERLY LOVE

I hated liver,

I hated peas,

I hated Baby Mike.

He ate my liver
and then my peas.

So now dumb Mike I like.

TIGHT SQUEEZE

Today I made a big mistake,
and I feel like a boob.

My sister asked, "How do they get
the toothpaste in the tube?"

Well, being a good sister,
I showed her.
After all, she is five (I am ten).

But she squeezed it so much
that I now need to know—

how to get the toothpaste in again.

LISTLESS WITH A LIST

I've just finished my Christmas list
of stuff I want this year:
CDs, games, and software disks;
I typed it so it's clear.
I've been a good kid every day.
While waiting I might burst!

Where IS Santa and his sleigh?
It's January twenty-first!

LETTERS

We have a VCR,
a DVD,
a CD-ROM,
an MP3,
an IBM,
a flat TV.
And we all live
(where else?)—
D.C.

Click!
Flip!
Nick.
Flip flip!
E!
Flip flip flip flip!
TNT.
Flip flip!

REMOTELY
BUSY

Showtime.
Flip flip!
WE.
Flip!
Food Network
fricassee!
Flip!
All-News!
Flip flip!
Fuse!
Flip flip flip flip!
Fox.
Flip flip flip flip!
Flip flip flip flip!
Flip flip!
Click!
Xbox!

WHAT'S THE POINT?

I'm sharpening my pencil.
I'm sharpening my pencil.
I'm sharpening my pencil.
I'm sharpening my pencil.
I'm sharpening my pencil.
I'm sharpening my pencil.
I'm sharpening my pencil.
I'm sharpening my pe . . .
Anybody want a pointy eraser?

SHOP TILL WE STOP

Shopping trip!
Fun galore!
I touched every
single thing
in the store!

I hid in the clothes racks
and rearranged prices.
Now that section is where
the two-cent merchandise is.

Some mannequins joined me
and we jumped on the beds.
The clerk lost his temper
when a few lost their heads.

The sporting goods section—
well, there's nothing to say.
They shouldn't keep baseballs
near the crystal display.

The store soon looked like
a hurricane hit it.
'Cause I wasn't watching,
I don't know who did it.

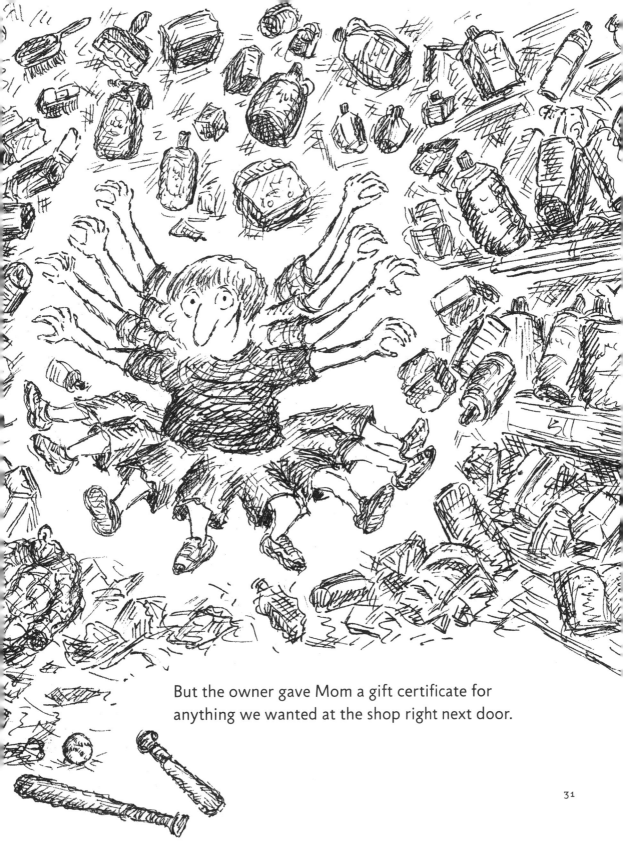

But the owner gave Mom a gift certificate for anything we wanted at the shop right next door.

WHOSE SIDE
ARE YOU ON?

The kids all call me "tattletale."
A blabbing,
crabbing
creature.
And if they do it
one more time . . .

I'm gonna
tell
the
teacher!

UNDER A SPELL

i c you're in a spelling b.
Well, good for u
and golly g.
Before it starts,
have some iced t.
And please do not
forget to p.

STUFF TO REMEMBER

A ball,
a fish,
a bus,
a cold
are all things that you catch.
A plan,
an egg,
a baby chick
are all things that you hatch.
An ice-cream cone,
your lips,
a pop
are all things that you lick.
If you see something green fly by,
watch out—I pick and flick.

CLAUS
CHASE

Santa is such a great guy,
and he's got special power.
'Cause we were in a motor home
Goin' fifty miles an hour.

As we roared down the highway,
I begged my dad, "Go slow."
'Cause overhead I heard a man
yelling, "Ho ho ho ho whoa!"

Dad pulled off at the exit,
and a booming voice
remarked,
"Merry Christmas,
here's your gifts—
and next year,
please stay parked!"

IN BRIEF...

"Change your underwear!
Change your underwear!"
Each day I hear Mom whine.

I tell her I do.
My brother does too.

I change into his,
he takes mine.

BUS FUSS

My sister is five.
It's her first day of school.
We wait for the bus,
and everything's cool.

Then tears!
Gushing tears!
Loud whimpering
and sobs!
Gushy things pour from the nose
(gobs and gobs)!

I did my best to cheer her
and help her to stay calm.
I said, "She'll be back this afternoon!
So please stop crying, Mom!"

TEMPER
TANTRUM

I'm not angry.
I'm not mad.
I'm not irate.
I'm not upset.
I'm not annoyed.
I'm not P.O.'d.
But if you're
curious,
I'd say . . .

I'm
furious.

THE DAILY
SNOOZE

When Grandpa's napping,
he starts to drool.
If I don't wake him soon,
we'll have a new pool!

EVERYBODY
COMMA DOWN!

The English teacher was in pain
while teaching punctuation.
He had to end the PERIOD
with pain and aggravation.
"My stomach hurts," he said in QUOTES.
"I think it's really swollen."
He DASHed for surgery, and now—
he has a SEMICOLON.

AFRAID OF
THE GRADE

1 is B
and 2 is A.
Then A, A, B, C, B.

The way I've guessed
on this whole test,
I can B sure I'll C A D!

OF MEALS AND SQUEALS

Our dinner table is loud.
My sister yells,
"More shells!"
My brother shouts,
"More sprouts!"
My sister booms,
"Legumes!"
My brother cries,
"More fries!"
My sister roars,
"More s'mores!"
They both utter,
"Butter!"

And I guess I'll eat later . . .
'cause they made me
the waiter.

UM . . .

People with bubble gum . . .
chew some.
People with coffee grounds . . .
brew some.
People with tomatoes . . .
stew some.
People with baseballs . . .
threw some.
People with crayons . . .
drew some.
People with bad colds . . .
blew some.
People with gooey tissues . . .
gruesome.

A LITTLE
RATTLED

We've got a new baby
at our house
to tickle
and cuddle
and coddle.
The baby says, "Goo goo."
And I say, "Blech!"

(That's the last time
I'm tasting his bottle!)

WORST
THINGS
FIRST

Mommy said no,
and then I asked Dad.

Daddy said yes;
now Mommy is mad.

So Daddy said no,
and Mommy agreed.

Them working together's
the last thing I need.

HOLD THE PUNCH, PLEASE

When the conductor punched
Dad's train ticket,
Dad smiled from ear to ear.
But when I punched
my baby brother,
Dad said no TV all year.

FEVER ACHIEVER

I've got a thermometer in my mouth
because Mom says I'm sick. It
is better to have it north than south
(where she wanted to stick it!).

A TALE WELL TOAD

I put froggy in my back pocket,
and he croaked
as loud as he could.
But when I forgot
and sat on a rock,
poor froggy
croaked
for good.

SET FOR LIFE

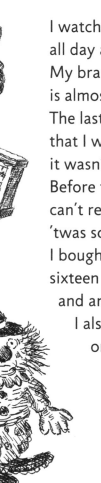

I watched TV
all day and night.
My brain
is almost gone.
The last two hours
that I watched,
it wasn't even on.
Before that,
can't remember . . .
'twas some kind of shopping thing.
I bought two vases,
sixteen clocks,
  and an engagement ring.
    I also watched a special
      on the making of a show
        about the making of a special
        special making of a show.
        I think I saw some cartoons
        running back to back for hours,
        with a clown who didn't laugh
        and a sheep with magic powers.

I know I should watch less TV,
and I will soon learn how,
'cause that's the talk-show subject
on a program starting now.

THE SHOWER

I'm gonna wash behind each ear
because I use them both to hear.
I'm gonna wash around my nose
because it breathes

(it also blows).

But I won't wash my belly button
because, you see,
it don't do
nuttin'.

WAKE-UP CALL

I was dreaming that
I was dreaming—
it happened just last night.
The strange thing is,
one dream was in color;
the other was black and white.
I had a nightmare that
I had a nightmare—
both woke me from my sleep.
Perhaps it was 'cause of those hairy monsters
I'd counted instead of sheep.

ON THE AIR!

A couch potato went to watch TV,
but he didn't use his smarts.

He plopped down without
looking first;
now the channels change
each time
he farts.

A SLICE OF LIFE . . .

Dad wanted to go camping.
Mom wanted to see Rome.
Deciding which to choose
was hard.

They debated the subject.
And then they compromised.
We ate pizza in the
backyard.

A SMASHING PRESENT

My brother's birthday gifts,
alas—
I made a big boo-boo.
I shook 'em hard,
and one was glass. . . .
Hope
someone
gives him
glue.

ONE, TWO, THREE, FORECAST

How's the weather in Philly?
Chilly.

How's the weather in Maine?
Rain.

How's the weather in Tampa?
Damper.

How 'bout other places in Florida?
Horrider.

You're such a bad weather fella.
Be quiet and take this umbrella.

CONTRACTION
DISSATISFACTION

It wasn't isn't.
It isn't wasn't.
It can't be shouldn't.
It shouldn't be doesn't.
It mustn't be wouldn't.
It wouldn't be mustn't.
It mayn't be mightn't.
It mightn't be mayn't.
I'm skipping this homework
to go out and playn't.

HAPPY BIRTHDAY
TO ME?

I was born in May.
Or June, perhaps.
It might have been
November.
The truth is,
I was very young;
I simply
don't remember.

THE **ONLY**
THING GOING OUT
IS THE LIGHT

Dad's in the car,
and Mom's getting dressed.
In her boudoir
Mom's primping her best.
Late's what they are,
and Dad's getting stressed.

Him waiting
she's keeping,
he's beeping
he's weeping
he's sleeping.

But do not feel sorrow—
they'll try again
tomorrow.

AUTO-MATICALLY PROBLEMATIC

Mom got a new car,
so no drinks in the back.
No markers,
no crayons,
and no crunchy snack.
No ice cream,
no pudding,
no putty,
no clay.
No feet on the seats
and no silly horseplay.
No toys filled with liquid
and nothing with chalk.

Good luck with the car, Mom,
but I'd rather walk.

NO SALE

I put my brother on eBay,
but nobody made a bid.
Perhaps it's 'cause I listed him
as "A Really Stinky Kid."

I knew it'd be hard to sell him,
but not quite as hard as this.
I think I'd better lower the price . . .
and maybe throw in our sis.

GIVE PIECE A CHANCE

I've been chewing this gum
for twenty-four weeks.
My lips are all numb
and so are my cheeks.
It has no more flavor,
it's no longer chewy.
And so at this time

I must say, PTUI!

HYGIENE!

Every night Gene brushes his teeth—
the ones on top,
the ones beneath.

When Gene's all foamy, then he quits.
And we all stand back
as he
spits!

VEXED AT THE MULTIPLEX

I had a jumbo bag of popcorn,
a soda, and some chips,
a box of gooey gumdrops
(and two very sticky lips).
A bar with coconut and fudge,
and lotsa sticky parts.
I'm really full,
and I can't wait
until the movie starts.

THE NAME'S THE SAME

In U.S. cities
and plenty of towns,
people have names
that are verbs and are nouns.

Gene wears jeans
and Jim's at the gym.
Mark makes his mark
(that's a homonym).

Skip and Flip know
what to do without fail.
But if your name's Rob,
then you're goin' to jail.

ON THE BALL

The first time you go bowling,
here's some things you've got to know:
Pick a ball that's not too heavy,
one you can swing to and fro.

Then slowly step up to the lane,
and stand there like a pro.
Then walk,
walk,
walk and fling that ball . . .

but remember to
let
go!

TEA-WRECKS

We were touring in London
when Dad said he thought
a spot of tea wouldn't hurt.
The teapot was
hot,
which Daddy
forgot,
and the spot of tea
covered his shirt.

SQUIDDING AROUND

Don't know anybody named Larry,
although I sure wish that I did.
It seems to me
that Larry is
a pretty good name for a kid.

Don't know any mollusks named Harry,
although I sure wish that I did.
It seems to me
that Harry is
a pretty good name for a squid.

By any chance is your name Larry?
If not, do you know of a kid
who calls himself Larry
and happens to have
a Harry-named pet who's a squid?

FRANCE-Y THAT

Do French flies
eat French fries?
And does it embarrass
if they are caught dining
on plaster of Paris?
Below my beret
all these questions remain.
Of French flies
and French fries
I'm going in-Seine!

WHAT A
(SEVENTH INNING)
STRETCH!

Baseball fans are crazy,
and you might say unaware.
They sing,
"Take me out to the ball game,"
   when they are
     already
       there.

STAY TUNED

I wish I could affordian
a really good accordion.
Each time I'd play a chordian
the people would applaudian.
Or someday I could be-anist
a famous solo pianist.
Or maybe play uponica
a beautiful harmonica.
Until then, I'm afraidio
I'll have to play the radio.

KINDER-GARDENING

When you try to trim a tree,
you should shoot for symmetry.
Cut too much
and you've got grief—
branches bare
beyond be-leaf.

A VISIT . . . OR IS IT?

I am going to the doctor.
But I am NOT
getting a shot.
Not me.
No way.
No how.

Ow!

CLASS TRIP

When Sinbad sailed the seven seas,
his cheeks were red and ruddy.
But when Sue brought home seven C's,
Mom kept her home to study.
The moral of this story is:
Folks cheer for exploration.
But you're not going anywhere
without an education.

WHAT A CATCH!

I tried to teach my pup
to fetch.
He could not get
the knack.
So now I throw my boomerang
and it brings doggie back!

WHY? HUH? WHY?

Why doesn't cough
rhyme with rough?
And same thing with
trough
and enough?
It's all so confusing!
From now on
I'm choosing
to skip this ridiculous
stough.

ANYBODY GOT A LIME?

I cannot think of a single rhyme.
I have this problem all the time.
If you'd help, I'd pay a dime
because this is an uphill climb.
My teacher's request is a crime—
she oughta know by now that I'm
not any good at words that rhyme.

REEL
TROUBLE

"You'll never catch a fish,"
Bill says.
Big brothers are such a pain.
But I have faith, and so I'll sit
and I will not complain.

"You won't catch a bass!
You won't catch a trout!"
Bill says, just trying to spoil it.
"You cannot catch a thing," he yells.
"You're fishing in the toilet!"

PAGE RAGE

My dad said,
"Turn off that TV!

"Sit down and read,"
he sighed.

I listened to him
and so, you see,
I'm reading TV GUIDE!

ICE
SCREAM

One scoop!
More!
Two scoops!
More!
Three scoops!
More!
Four sc . . . oops!
Floor!

MONEY
MATTERS

I saved all my pennies
and soon had a nickel.
I saved all my nickels
and soon had a dime.
I saved all my dimes
and soon had a quarter.
I saved all my quarters
and went to the store.

Yes, I'd saved and saved for a video system,
which really was quite an expense.
But the clerk looked down and laughed in my face . . .

I only had eighty-three cents.

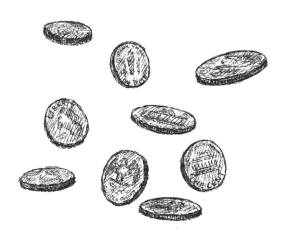

A CLEAN BETTER IDEA

Mom would be proud—
I washed my hands.
Of that I'm fairly certain.
Though it's not allowed,
I understand,
to wipe 'em
on
the
curtain!

THE SAD TRUTH

This poem has no rhythm,
it's just a
silly verse.
If you thought the one
on the last page
was bad,
the next one's sure to be
worse!

THE **REAR** WIPER

I do not mean to be upset.
I don't mean to be hyper.
But Dad told me he had to get
himself a new rear wiper.

"Rear wipers are for tots," I said.
He let the comment pass.
"I'll pick one up," he said instead,
"the next time I get gas."

But wait, the tale goes on from there;
what he said next was freaky:
"Perhaps I ought to buy a pair
to keep from getting streaky!"

I said to Dad, "What do you mean?
This whole thing is bizarre!"
He said, "The wiper is to clean
the rear glass on my car."

It turned out that the wiper would
keep Dad's back window shiny.
I'm happy now; he never should
use that thing on his heiny!

ALL ABOUT US

My dad's a veterinarian.
My mom is a librarian.
They both are vegetarian.
My sister's name is Marian.

I'm Dave; I'm an Aquarius.
I play the Stradivarius.

And that is everything I know.
I've said enough.
You'd better go!

NOT QUITE
SITTING PRETTY

I had some gas
while in church class,
but what else could I do?
I said,
"Alas,
it's an impasse,"

and sat there in
the pew.

OOPS!

I did something bad,
and Mom's angry;
she says that she's gonna tell Dad.

It's been a bad week
for behavior;
this problem's the third
that I've had.

And Daddy will surely believe her;
it's a case that we've already proved.
So I'm putting a sign on the front door:
HIYA, DAD, DON'T COME IN,
'CAUSE WE'VE MOVED!

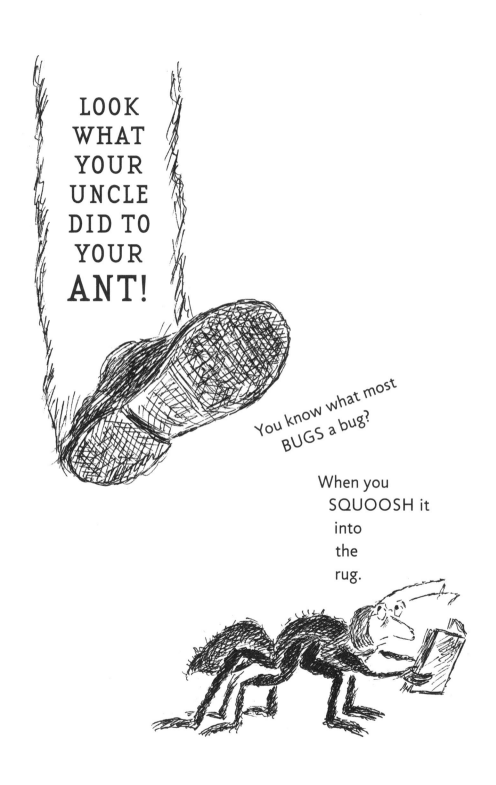

LOOK
WHAT
YOUR
UNCLE
DID TO
YOUR
ANT!

You know what most
BUGS a bug?

When you
SQUOOSH it
into
the
rug.

A BAD AT BAT AT THAT

If I get a double,
we win the game.
I'm facing
Fast-Pitch Frankie.
Strike one!
Strike two!
Oh, what a shame!

Has someone got
a hankie?

READY FOR COLLEGE
(OR IS THAT **COLLAGE?**)...

Don't taste paste.
Don't chew glue.
I learned so much
on the first day of school—
what more could they teach
on day two?

'SNOT WHERE YOU START . . .

Picking your nose is very wrong;
it's a fact that for years
I have known.
So don't worry,
that's something I will never do . . .
instead I'll keep picking my own.

CUT IT OUT!

Dad cuts coupons from the paper.
Kitty Yummies for a quarter—
how 'bout that!

He bought a lot and saved, saved, saved.
It's too bad we don't have a cat!

Mom said, "Honey, we don't need them!"
Dad answered, "I won't take them back!"

Warning: If you come to our house,
say NO if Dad offers a snack!

I NEED SOME
SOUND
ADVICE

DRIP, DROP,
plop!
Drip, drop,
PLOP!
All night it keeps me awake.
DRIP, DROP,
plop!
Drip, drop,
PLOP!
Don't know how much I can take.
DRIP, DROP,
PLOP!
Drip, drop,
PLOP!
It just constantly flows.
Drip, DROP,
plop!
Drip, drop, PLOP!

My stupid sister
and her leaky nose!

THE REAL DEAL
ABOUT THE MEAL

Peas porridge hot,
peas porridge cold.
Peas porridge in the pot
nine days old.

Peas porridge hot,
peas porridge cold.
We ordered Chinese food
'cause the pot
was full of mold!

MY REPORT CARD

In every subject
I deserved
an A-plus
plus
plus
plus.

But that's not what
Miss Smith
observed.
Better leave this on the bus.

STEP ON IT
(OR MAYBE NOT)

Are we there yet?
I'm hungry.
Are we there yet?
I'm hungry.
Are we there yet?
I'm hungry.
I gotta pee.
Are we there yet?
I'm hungry.
I gotta pee.
Are we there yet?
I'm really hungry.
I gotta pee.

Are we there yet?
I'm really hungry.
I really gotta pee.
Are we there yet?
I'm really hungry.
I really really gotta pee.
Are we there yet?
I'm really hungry.

Uh-oh.
Are we there yet?

TROUBLE IN PENCIL-VANIA

I don't know what a **verb** is,
but I'm RUNNING to find out.
I've no idea what they mean by a **noun**,
but I am a loyal SCOUT.
An **adjective** is something
that gives me a TICKLISH brain.
And an **adverb**'s a word
that seems quite absurd,
so I'm QUICKLY going

down the drain!

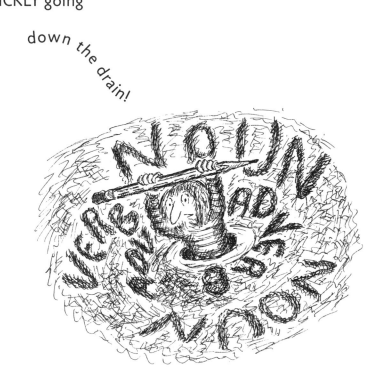

PUFF THE MAGIC UNCLE

The mumps I thought
my uncle had
for weeks and weeks and weeks,
I soon was taught
(thanks to my dad) . . .
he's just got
real fat cheeks.

CAN HE DRIVE HIM
HOME?

Dad got lost
on the way to the game.
On the radio
it was beginning.
He wouldn't ask
directions;

we got there
in the ninth inning.

CANDLE
WITH CARE

Every day's somebody's birthday.
If it's yours,
hurray!
(Ain't I nice?)
I don't have a present,
but 'cause I'm so pleasant,
have cake
and then save me
a slice.

THE FILLING'S **NOT** THRILLING

I wentist
to the dentist.
I shutist
my mouthist.
He drillist,
I squirmist.
He tryist,
I cryist.
Good-byeist.

MY WORD!

I never know when to use TO
or use TOO.
I'm really bad figuring out
THREW
or THROUGH.
I get them wrong often
and no longer care,
though it would be fun
to be right
hear and their.

'TWAS THE DAY
BEFORE CHRISTMAS

I wanted toys!
I wanted toys!

Oh wait, that doesn't make sense.

I meant to say that I WANT toys.
I guess I'm "present tense."

JUST CALL ME MAGGIE

I'm Margaret McPherson McNally McBride.
I'm named for a cousin on my father's side.
And also an aunt
who was loved by my mother.
As well as some guy
who worked with Grandpa's brother.
I'm really surprised at what my parents did.
If they liked all those names,
should've had one more kid!

HALLWAY HIJINKS

An errand to the principal's office
is a really important job.
It's not an assignment a teacher gives
to a pay-no-attention slob.

So as I turn the corner,
I'm handling the task fine.
I pick up speed around the turn
and screech toward the finish line!

I hopscotch 'cross the tiles
and dive headlong into first;
get up and make the safe sign;
grab some water for my thirst.
I leap round Mrs. Jorgensen
and her rolling library cart,
then bash into the lockers
(which wasn't very smart).

An errand to the principal's office
can be a dangerous job
For me it was quite an adventure.
Next time I wish they'd send Bob.

FOOD FOR THOUGHT

Alphabet soup is really yummy.
I like when words go in my tummy.
It's consonants in consommé.
Watch what you spell,
watch what you say.
Last night I used it to
spell "poop,"
and Mom washed my
mouth out
with soup!

LONG DE-**VISION**

The doctor said,
"Read that eye chart . . .
line four,
please read it all."

I cannot see the chart,
to start—
'cause I
can't see the wall.

A RATTY
THING TO DO

If you want to get your sister
to run
screaming
out of the house,
switch around her
computer
and plug in

a live mouse.

SEE YA . . .

This is the final poem in the book,
which makes me really blue.
I feel like we've gotten to know each other
as you took the time to read through.
I'll miss the way you turned the pages.
I'll miss your silly laughs.
I'll miss your happy face,
which I think looks like a giraffe's.

I hope you've liked my rhyming
as this book of poems ends.
And if you did, run out
and buy a million for your friends.
Be sure to tell your teachers;
this could help them when they teach.
And by the way, I should have said
get your friends a million EACH.
I hope that as you grow up,
this book often brings you joy—
because you are my absolutely
favorite girl
(or boy).

Okay, I will admit it—I just do not have a clue
if you read this book at all,
or if you're even you.
I do not know about you,
and I've never heard your laugh.

(Although I still do think that you look just like a giraffe!)

INDEX OF TITLES

INDEX OF FIRST LINES

SPECIAL BONUS PAGES!!

BONUS! BONUS!

so turn the page already . . .

OOPS!
There's More!

Congratulations, my friend! You are the one-billionth person to finish reading *Oops!*, and in gratitude, and at extremely great expense, I am sending you this very special page via ultradeluxe high-speed satellite.

This page—and the twenty-eight pages that follow—doesn't appear in anyone else's copy of *Oops!* What's more, the fact that *you* got these pages is truly a miracle of modern technology, because as you read this, the pages and words are being beamed at 45.3 kilobeams per second, which is roughly the speed of a hyper-launched sneeze on a lunar module careening through outer space.

And wait'll you see what's next! You've won a brand-new . . .

Okay, I lied.

You are *not* the one-billionth person to read *Oops!*

You are *not* the only reader to get these extra pages.

I am *not* beaming anything to this book via satellite.

You haven't won anything.

And frankly, I totally made up the whole thing you just read.

But here's the deal. . . .

I got to the hundredth poem and I just didn't want to see this book come to an end.

Now, working with Ed Koren has been one of the greatest thrills of my life. He is so kind, so funny, so creative, and so wonderful. In fact, let's hear it for him:

"Hip, hip, hooray, Ed! Hip, hip, hooray, Ed! Hip, hip, hooray, Ed!"

Good, that was nice. I feel better. But there's still a problem: What does a poet do when he's got more to say, but he doesn't really want to bother his fantastic illustrator to do more illustrations?

A puzzlement, to be sure.

So, here's what I did.

I got up one morning and called Ed and I said, "Hey Ed, it's me. I've got more ideas. Let's keep worki . . ."

And he said, "Who is this? And why are you calling me at 3 a.m.?" Then he hung up.

I can't blame him. Listen, illustrators need their sleep.

So here's my plan: I'm gonna fill the following pages with important stuff, and as I'm writing, I'll call Ed back from time to time and see if he can help out.

Because one thing's for sure: *I* can't draw. Not at all. When I was a kid, no one knew what I was drawing. I'd show my pictures to relatives and they'd say, "Nice froggy." Or "Cute boat." And I'd say, "That's not a froggy! That's not a boat! That's a chicken dancing with a carrot in the middle of a schoolroom filled with ostriches doing a musical salute to Ben Franklin!"

Everyone thought my drawings were weird. And I thought they were weird for thinking I was weird. And they thought that I was weird for . . . Anyway, you get the idea. My parents were so proud of my pictures that they hung them all *inside* the refrigerator.

Even today, I can't draw to save my life (although that's probably not ever gonna come up—I can't imagine a doctor examining me and saying, "Mr. Katz, we can't operate. The only way to save your life is if you draw an adorable squirrel.") In fact, here's an example of my work as an adult—I've copied Ed Koren's incredible illustration from the cover of this book.

Sorry, Ed, I tried.

Seriously, that's my best attempt. I really mean it.

Writing is what I do. And it's what I've always done. Even as a first grader, all I wanted to do was write. Well, maybe I also wanted to be an astronaut—or perhaps even a rocket, based on this actual entry from my first-grade school "newspaper":

SAVED BY A FISHERMAN

One sunny afternoon, a little boy took a walk. Soon he came to a bridge. The bridge was over a stream. The boy walked over the small bridge and he fell through a hole in it. A fisherman was fishing on the bank of the stream and he heard the boy call for help. The fisherman saved his life.

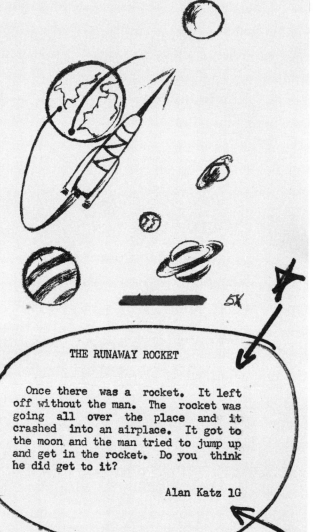

OUR TRIP

My sister and I went alone by bus to Washington, D.C. We played games on the bus with the hostess. We saw many important buildings. We had a good time visiting the places. I will always remember our trip and I hope I can go on another soon.

THE RUNAWAY ROCKET

Once there was a rocket. It left off without the man. The rocket was going all over the place and it crashed into an airplace. It got to the moon and the man tried to jump up and get in the rocket. Do you think he did get to it?

Alan Katz 1G

FUN WITH BLOCKS

We play with blocks in school. Sometimes we make roads. Sometimes we make buildings. I like to play with blocks because it is fun.

Kgn. 2

HOW WE DRAW IN SCHOOL

We make different color pictures in school. We paste and cut and draw. I like to draw because I like to make things.

Kgn. 2

As a second grader, I was writing funny stuff in class all the time. Once my teacher asked for a book report on "Jack and the Beanstalk." Instead, I wrote a parody of the story, in which Jack traded his cow for a color television instead of magic beans. My teacher laughed nervously, then asked some very important questions, such as "He wanted a color TV for his family's tenth-floor two-bedroom apartment in Queens—but where had they been keeping the cow that he traded?" She also wanted to know what happened to the beanstalk part, since that kind of was the point of the whole story.

Alan
PS179Q
Mrs. Bailowitz

Jack and the Beanstalk

Once upon a time there was
a Boy Named Jack he lived with
his mom and their cow in a 10th Floor
one Room apartment. One Day, mom
sed "Jack plese Be a good Boy
and Bring the cow to market and trade
her For vegetables and other good Foods."

Jack sed "But mom, cant we kepe her?
She is a good Friend and she moos me
to slep evre night."

But mom sed No and so he went to morket
and traded the cow For Beans which
he that were Beans to eat But wate
were really magic Beans instead.

then he traded the magic Beans for what
he really wanted — a color tv.

Wen he got home his mother was mad,
she sed "you cant eat a color tv."

and Jack sed "No But you cant watch
vegetables".

Jack was sent to his Room For 3 weeks
But he didint mind Beakos the color
tv was in there to.

I don't remember what I told the teacher, but looking back, it's pretty clear to me that my teachers just didn't get my humor. In fact, here's my actual third-grade report card—take a look at my teacher's comment:

IMM—10/66

BOARD OF EDUCATION
CITY OF NEW YORK

Public School _179_   Borough _Queens_

REPORT TO PARENTS

GRADES 2-6

September 19_66_   June 19_67_

Name of Pupil _Alan Katz_

Class _5/4 - 20 8_   Room _20 8_

~~Miss~~
Mrs.   _Eleanor Diamond_
Name of Teacher ~~Mr.~~   _Celia Smith_

Dear Parents,

The purpose of this report is to tell you how your child is getting along in school. You will receive reports three times a year.

No two children are exactly alike. This is a report about your child's achievement in school.

During the course of the year, your child will be given standardized tests. The results of these tests will be available to you upon request.

You are urged to make comments in the space provided. If you have any question, please feel free to arrange a conference with your child's teacher. Please sign and return this report promptly.

Cordially yours,

Principal

Teacher Comments

Period 1 *Alan must work towards expressing his written ideas more creatively.*

Period 2 *Alan can do very well in all the subject areas but he can join in class discussions more.*

Period 3 *May you have a healthy and worthwhile summer.*

Parent Comments

Period 1

Parent's Signature ___ Mrs S. Katz

Period 2

Parent's Signature ___ Mrs S. Katz

New Grade and Room ___ 6/5 - 213

First Day of New Term ___ 9/11/67

4

I remember that teacher once slammed the blackboard so hard with her fist that she actually broke it (the blackboard, not the fist)! From then on, she had to scrunch the assignments so they fit on the non-cracked part of the board. I remember thinking that was hysterical, but now I'm not so sure.

Anyway, I got through school by writing funny stuff, even when the assignment didn't call for it. Now, I'm certainly not recommending that *you* do that, but it kind of worked for me.

Here's a piece I wrote in fourth grade about the famous sixteenth-century astronomer Galileo. The teacher was clearly expecting a serious report, but instead I handed in this poem:

> Galileo gave us stars.
> He also gave us hope.
> He helped us know the Moon from Mars
> with his great telescope.

He was the first of all to check.

The first to wonder why.

He was the first to tilt his neck

and say, "Hey look, the sky!"

Although totally not based on scientific fact (I'm pretty sure now that Galileo wasn't the first person ever to look up), the teacher was impressed. Sort of. She gave me an A+ for my writing and a D for my art. Here's my art:

As my school years passed, I wrote funny stuff whenever I could. I once won a savings bond from a sneaker company for writing a poem about how Paul Revere could've gotten around town faster if he'd worn their sneakers instead of riding a horse. Again, totally not based on fact. Oops.

I contributed a lot of material to the school newspapers. For some reason, I enjoyed writing a ton of trivia, as you can see here:

Books of The Times

The members of the Library Club have contributed the following articles.

Acrostics

Practically Seventeen was about a
        girls problem,
Real excitement and sadness,
A truly wonderful book.
Cheerful Tobey's holiday, is disaster,
Tobey's friend, Brase, ignores her.
It ends happily for Tobey.
Crickety Midge, reads Tobey's diary,
Angry outburst from Tobey.
Livid with anger,
Later grateful to Midge.
You will enjoy Tobey as a mediator.

Suddenly the wedding is called off.
Even Midge helps her.
Very soon Alicia and Adam are together,
Everything ends well with the wedding.
Now with four people left, it is lonely.
Tobey is never happier than when Brose
        gives her his ring.
Everyone will enjoy this book,
Especially the girls.
Never able to take your eyes off the
        book, until the very end.

Library Club

A	J	A	Y	W	I	L	L	I	A	M	S	R	O	N	P
Z	R	L	Y	S	I	R	N	T	Z	P	F	Q	S	A	L
H	P	T	O	Z	M	L	U	B	O	Z	L	D	G	I	M
J	A	N	E	L	A	N	G	T	O	N	J	W	R	R	O
I	Y	S	R	H	L	B	N	E	N	W	R	Q	J	N
Q	N	U	F	C	N	L	A	S	E	L	L	E	P	G	Q
K	C	L	T	H	R	O	B	C	R	T	S	O	N	V	R
J	W	X	Q	I	R	Z	V	X	Y	L	R	O	H	Z	S

Work horizontally, vertically and diagonally. Find the following popular authors.
        Keith Robertson, Jane Langton,
        J.B.Payne, Jay Williams,
        Fen Lasell

Library Club

Stories of Champions - Sam Ebstin
Match these men with their nicknames.

Ty Cobb -------- Sultan of Swat
Babe Ruth ------- The Georgia Peach
Honus Wagner --- The Say-Hey Kid
Willie Mays ---- The Big Six
Cristy Mathewson-Flying Dutchman

Answers

Mays	--	Say-Hey Kid
Ruth	--	Sultan of Swat
Wagner	--	The Flying Dutchman
Matheson	--	The Big Six
Johnson	--	The Big Train
Cobb	--	Georgia Peach

Alan Katz 6/5-213

BOOK REBUS

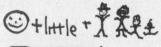

by
Happy Little Family

by
The King Who Could Not Smile

Barbara Hendlin
6-204

I also wrote plays and funny song lyrics for shows. And I kept writing ridiculous essays when serious material was called for.

I also joked my way through college (which didn't always please the professors). In fact, a couple of years ago I sang songs from my Silly Dilly books at an event in New York City, and one of my college professors was in the audience.

The minute I finished singing, with my off-key "Stinky Stinky Diaper Change" still filling the air (if you think I can't draw, you should hear me *sing*), I ran to where she was sitting and asked, "Can that count as the presentation I never did in my sophomore year of college?"

She said "no" and gave me a D and the phone number of a local singing teacher.

I just called Ed. He's taking a shower.

So it was no surprise when I chose as my career—comedy writing. Over the past twenty-five years, I've written comedy for network TV series and specials, game shows, animated series, awards shows, commercials, comic books, trading cards, and more. But guess what?

Out of everything I've ever done, writing books for kids is by far my favorite job.

You might've seen some of these Silly Dilly books:

- *Take Me Out of the Bathtub and Other Silly Dilly Songs*
- *I'm Still Here in the Bathtub: Brand New Silly Dilly Songs*
- *Where Did They Hide My Presents? Silly Dilly Christmas Songs*
- *Are You Quite Polite? Silly Dilly Manners Songs*

David Catrow did a wonderful job illustrating all of these books of wacky song parodies, and the feeling of holding an actual, finished book in your hands is, to me, the greatest in the world.

A few years ago, my Silly Dilly editor, Emma, asked if I could write poems to be read instead of sung. I thought back to all my years of rhyming (and all the kids, teachers, and parents who'd suffered through hearing me sing) and said sure, I'd try it.

So I did.

I grabbed my trusty rhyming dictionary (a MUST for anyone who's trying to write a poem or a song or anything that rhymes!) and sat down at my kitchen table to write. Over the years I've trained myself to write anywhere and on anything—poems from *Oops!* were composed in the library, on the New York City subway system, in the stands of a Little League field, on line at a bank, in bed, and in restaurants. One of the poems was even written in its entirety while I was on the potty. If you can guess which one, e-mail me at alankatzbooks@aol.com and I'll let you know if you're right.

Anyway, the first poem I wrote for this book was the first I'd attempted in about twenty years. And it was . . .

I've got a menomener in my mouf
Becuz mom sz I'm sick, it
is better to have it norf than souf,
where mom had wanned ta stick it!

I e-mailed it to Emma the editor, and she called and said, "What are you talking about?!!?!"

I explained that the poem was being read by a kid who had a thermometer in his or her mouth, so the words weren't so easy to understand. ("Mouf" = "mouth," get it?) And Emma, dear sweet editor that she is, explained right back that since you, the reader, probably wouldn't be reading this book with a thermometer in your mouth, it shouldn't be written that way.

So I revised the poem to read:

I've got a thermometer in my mouth
because Mom says I'm sick. It
is better to have it north than south
(where she wanted to stick it!).

That poem had a happy ending, so to speak, because
it made it into *Oops!* But there were other poems
along the way that didn't make it for one reason or
another. Here are two:

You say tom-ah-to,
I say tom-ay-to.
You say pot-ah-to,
I say pot-ay-to.
Now please . . .
take that tom-ay-to
and that pot-ay-to
off of my
plate-o!

And

I could go on reality TV:
Sleep in germs,
and eat worm
marmalade.
I could take all the worst,
but somehow,
gotta first
find a way to survive
in third grade.

Editing is part of every good writing task, and I agreed when Emma suggested we leave those two poems out of the book. So they're not here. Hope you enjoyed them.

(If you see Emma, please don't tell her they're in the book after all. In exchange, I will send you one billion dollars.)

Okay, I lied.

I won't send you anything. Though if you ever e-mail me, I will e-mail you back with a poem.

Which poem?

I have no idea, because it'll be one I haven't written yet. But it'll be great and you'll love it, I promise.

And then you can print it out and show all your friends and say, "Look what *I* wrote!"

No, wait, I'm kidding. Don't do that. Seriously. Show it to your friends and say, "Look what Alan Katz wrote for me." Because, really, I'll be the only one who'll be able to say "Look what *I* wrote!" about that specific poem.

But do you know what? (Say, "No, Alan, what?")

Here's what: I would love it if you'd write your own poems. It's not hard to do and it's great fun. You can write a poem about most anything: people you know, places you've been, stuff you own, stuff you want, things you like and things you don't, and so on. Or you can dip into your imagination and make up characters, items, and such.

You could even write a poem about writing a poem. Or *not* writing a poem—like the following, written especially for this occasion:

> By the time I
> finish my
> poetry,
> you could go out
> and
> grow a tree.

Or

> Baby brother's hair: shampooable
> Mom's library book: renewable
> Dad's morning coffee: brewable
> Little sister's vitamin: chewable
> Me writing a poem: undoable

I just called Ed Koren and he says he's not home.

So, where was I? Oh yeah, writing poems. It's something you should do. And do again. And again. And again. And if you do it one hundred times and put together a collection, I'll read it—just like you read my book of poems. Just do me a favor and don't call it *Oops!* (Or *Uh-Oh!*, which is what my next collection of poems with Ed Koren is probably going to be called.) In fact, that brings up an interesting point. At least it's interesting to me, and I hope it'll be interesting to you, should I ever stop this sentence and actually get around to telling you the point that was interesting to me in the first place. Here it is:

Books can be hard to write, but they're even harder to title. This book had about twelve different titles before we came up with *Oops!* They include:

Tattletale

One, Two, Three Forecast

Tea-Wrecks

Wash Behind Each Ear

Stuff to Remember

Everybody Comma Down

I'm Out of the Bathtub and I've Got Some
    Time to Rhyme

Now you know why we chose *Oops!*

And as I told you before, the next collection is probably going to be called *Uh-Oh!* And after that, who knows? In fact, that could be a good title: *Who Knows?* We'll see. But at this point, I'm totally open to suggestions.

Emma just called. She asked me to do two things.

1. Stop bothering Ed Koren.
2. End this book.

As for #1, I understand. But when it comes to #2, once again, that makes me sad. I love being a poet and I love that you've taken the time to make it all the way through to this page. And so seeing as I'm officially out of pages, I'll say good-bye for now, thanks for everything, and . . .

"Hip, hip, hooray for you!

Hip, hip, hooray for you!

Hip, hip, hooray for you!"

Bye!

self-portrait